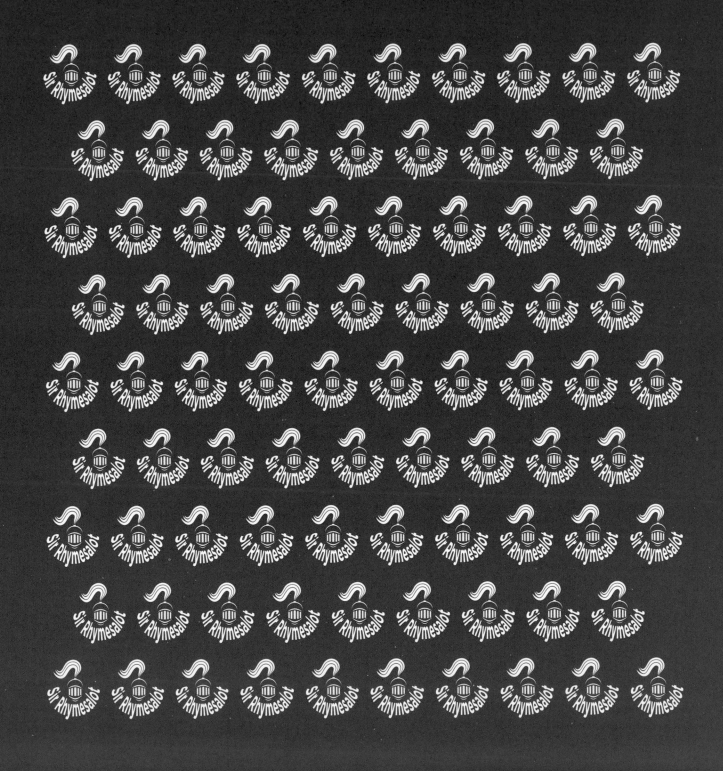

I LOST MY TIRED

Whatever you do, don't turn on the lights

Sir Rhymesalot

This book contains rhyming Tools. Scan the QR code to find out how they work.

Under the covers,
what a great place to be

Wrapped up and snuggly
at a quarter to three

I'm not quite awake
and I'm not quite asleep

Quietly over the covers I peep

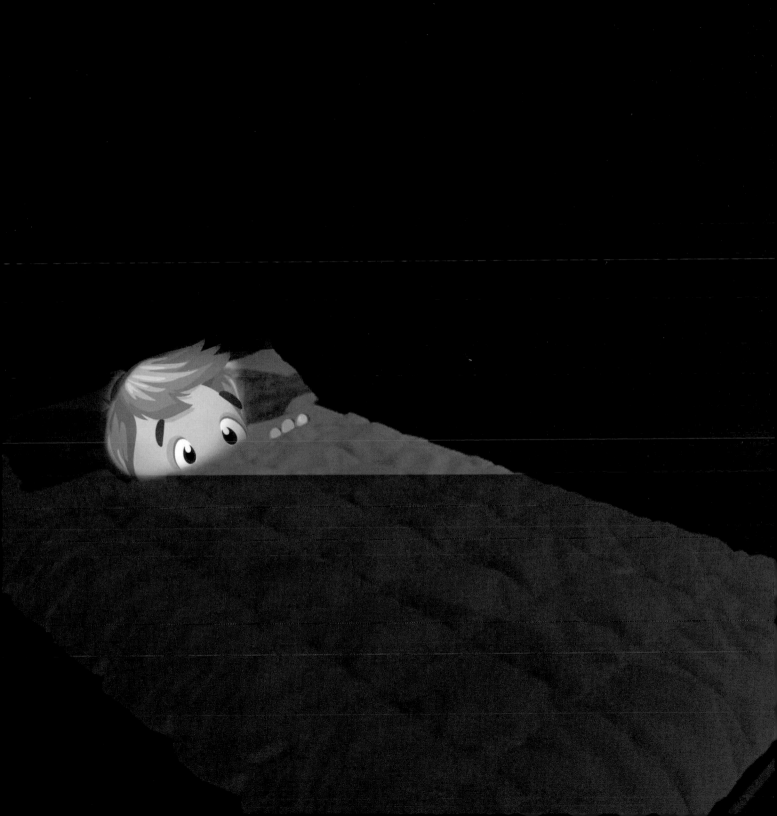

That pizza for dinner
made my thirsty get big

Three waters, two juices,
and an iced tea I swigged

That fifth glass of milk
was too much, no doubt

Now it's done going though me,
and it wants to get out

I slide out one foot,
I can feel the cold night

The bathroom is far,
three doors on the right

Twenty-two steps
'tween me and relief

Then twenty-two back
to my cozy warm sheets

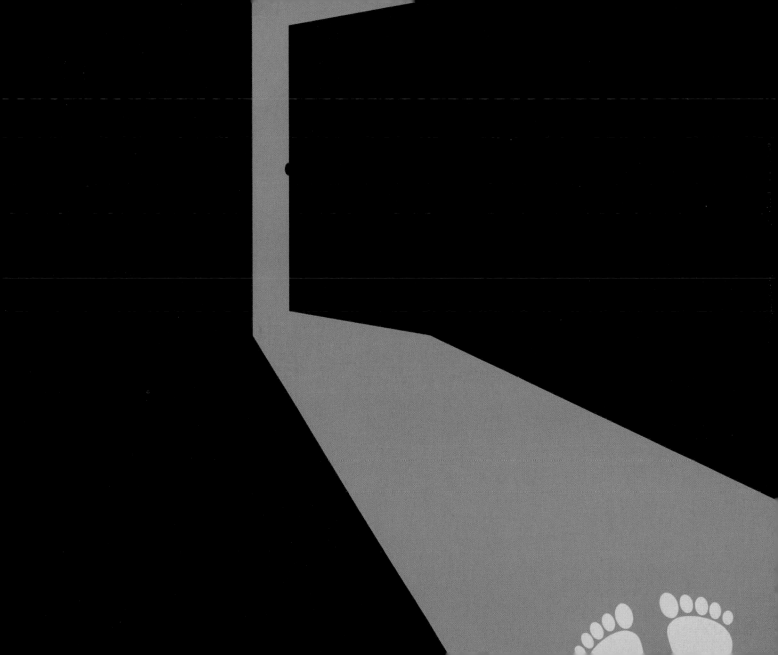

But this is just where
the problems begin

Not the cold nor the distance,
cause my chagrin

I must make the trip
to do what's required

But when I get back,
I'll have lost all my tired

Right now, I can slip
back to sleep in an instant

If it wasn't for this liquid
whose exit's insistent

I've been in the snoozes
since my cheeks hit the sheets

I wish I could 'go'
and go right back to sleep

Slowly I slink,
my toes meet the floor

Searching for slippers,
one toe and then four

Hastily, shakily,
step after **step**

How endless and friendless
a hallway can **get**

Mindfully, finally
I reach the big bowl

Slowly and flowly
I relax my control

It seems to take ages,
time standing **still**

My tired is escaping,
awakeness I **feel**

Now come the thoughts,
excited for morning

I can't make them stop,
the new day is calling

I'll eat up my breakfast,
pancakes are my favorite

One bite at a time,
with syrup I'll savor it

A toasty warm shower,
quick-quick, I'll be late

Then out to the car where
my chauffeur awaits

I call mom my chauffeur,
it gives her a **giggle**

Into the **deep** leather seat
my butt **wiggles**

Then off down the road
in the shiny machine

It's not far to school,
not far to Marlene

Marlene is my friend,
the girl of my dreams

If I could be king,
I'd make her my queen

But wait, hold the boat,
let's think this again

It was Friday last night
so today's the weekend

Now I'm excited
in a doubly way

But I'm twice as awake
as I am in the day

I hop off the seat
and pull up my shorts

Then it dawns in my head,
"It's Saturday sports!"

I've got to get sleep,
I must play at my **best**

Marlene will be watching,
now I am **stressed**

Back down the hall, in bed I hop
Empty I am, but sleepy I'm not

I knew it would happen,
I shouldn't have started

I'm fully awake, my tired has departed

I count to one hundred and then I count sheep
I count all the miles between me and sleep

I just want my tired, I just want my dreams
Oh no, now it's worse,
I'm counting Marlenes

Maybe I'll read,
sometimes that helps

I reach up and pull down
a book from my shelf

What's this new book
mommy said I would love?

I've lost my tired,
but he's lost his hug

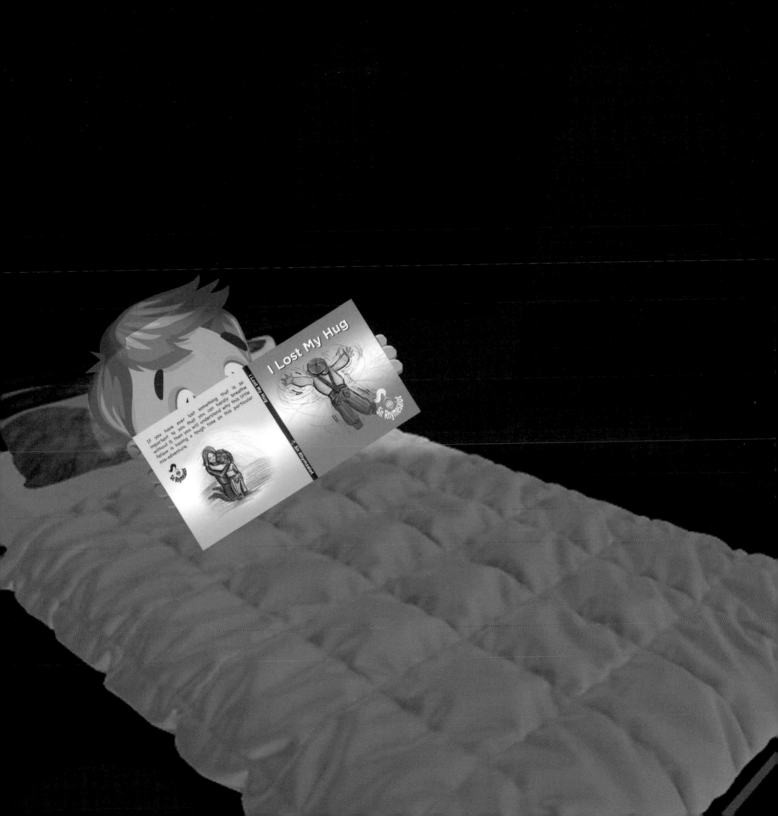

I read and I read,
trying to escape

I do love this book
but it's now super late

It just doesn't help,
I tried and I tried

My sleepy has left me,
I can't find my tire...zzzzzzz

And he slept all night

Scan this QR code with your phone camera for more titles from imagine and wonder

Your guarantee of quality

As publishers, we strive to produce every book to the highest commercial standards. The printing and binding have been planned to ensure a sturdy, attractive publication which should give years of enjoyment.

Replacement assurance
If your copy fails to meet our high standards, please inform us and we will gladly replace it.
admin@imagineandwonder.com

Printed in China by Hung Hing Off-set Printing Co. Ltd.

Scan the QR code to find other
Sir Rhymesalot books and more from
www.ImagineAndWonder.com

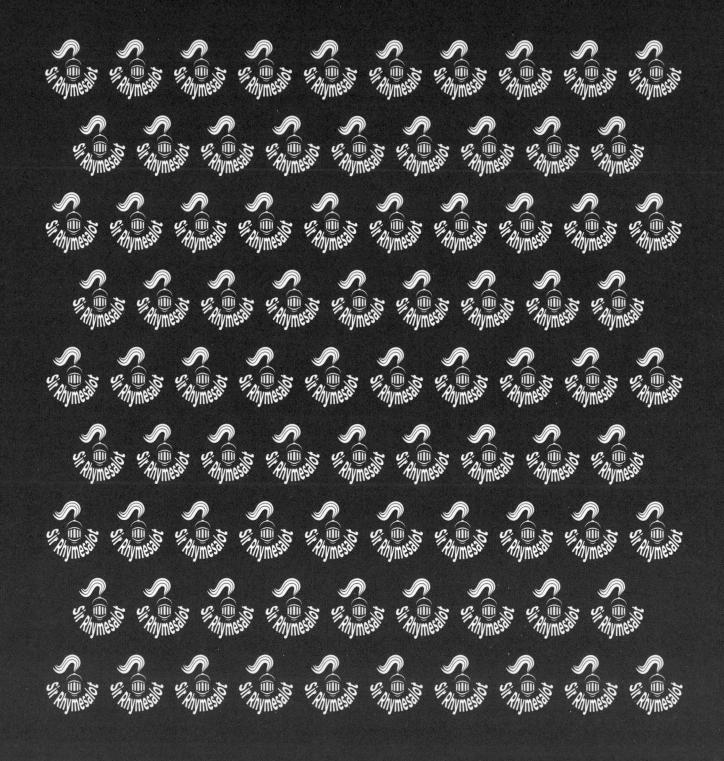